A Look at
Spiders

Written by Jerald Halpern

STECK-VAUGHN
ELEMENTARY · SECONDARY · ADULT · LIBRARY

A Harcourt Classroom Education Company

www.steck-vaughn.com

Contents

What Is a Spider?

    Some people think that spiders are insects, but they are not. Both spiders and insects have a hard covering on the outside of their bodies. Spiders have eight legs and no wings. Insects have six legs and usually do have wings.

pincher

head

leg

body

spinnerets

All spiders have the same body parts. The main part of their body is divided into two sections. In the front, there are eight legs and two pinchers. Special parts in the back, called **spinnerets,** make **silk**. Spiders use the silk to make **webs**.

Spiders have five senses. Their sense of touch is the strongest. They can feel anything that moves near them. They use their mouth and front pinchers to taste and smell food. To see, most spiders have eight eyes. Spiders have small openings on their legs to help them hear sounds.

How Big Are Spiders?

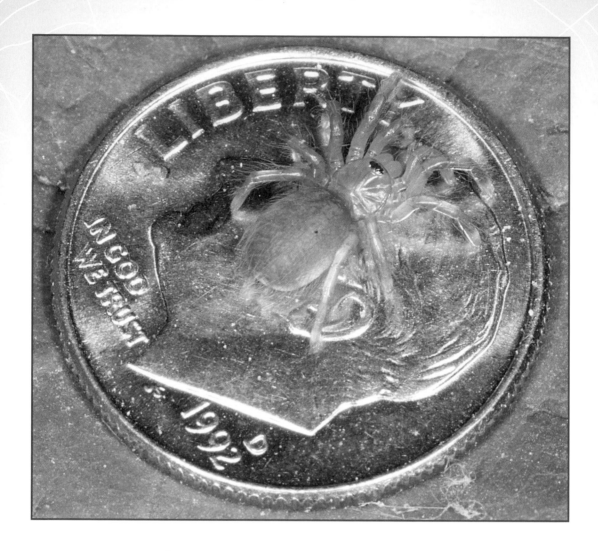

Spiders can be very large. They can even grow bigger than an adult's hand. But spiders can also be much smaller. Some never get bigger than the top of a pin. Female spiders are always larger than male spiders.

Tarantulas are the largest spiders in the world. Those found in South America can be as long as a sheet of paper. Comb-footed spiders are the smallest spiders. They can be as small as the point of a pencil.

Where Do Spiders Live?

Spiders live in many places. They live at the top of mountains or on the bottom of caves. Some live in damp areas. Others live in deserts. Some spiders live on the ground, some in trees, and some in buildings.

The water spider lives in a pond. It makes a silk home on underwater plants. The spider traps a bubble of air and brings it below to its home. This is how the spider can breathe while in the water.

Most spiders live in silk webs they have built. Some webs have a round shape. Some webs have a zigzag look, and some look like tents. A spider's web is amazing to see.

How Do Spiders Make Silk?

Spiders make silk inside their bodies. It is squeezed out like toothpaste through the spinnerets. The silk is like thread that gets hard. Spiders use their silk in different ways.

Most spiders use their silk to **weave** a
web. But not all spiders make webs. Some
use silk to make a bed on a leaf. Others
use silk to line **tunnels** in the ground.
Many spiders use silk to wrap up insects
so they can eat them later.

How Do Spiders Eat?

Spiders have a strange way of eating. They turn their food into a liquid. Then they drink the liquid. It is like drinking milk through a straw!

13

Spiders are picky eaters. They usually eat only insects. Sometimes they may eat small frogs or lizards. First they trap the **prey** in their web. Then they **poison** it with a bite.

What Kinds of Spiders Are There?

There are many different kinds of spiders. Spiders can be different in color and in size. They can also be different in the ways they move and how they hunt for their prey.

Tarantulas are very large and hairy. They are the biggest of all the spiders. Tarantulas use sharp **fangs** to bite and kill their prey. They can also shed their long hairs to poison their prey.

Jumping spiders have short legs, but they are able to jump very far. Two of their legs are used just for jumping. These spiders jump to sneak up on insects. They jump again to catch them.

Trap-door spiders dig tunnels in the ground. They line the tunnels with silk they have spun. Then the spiders make a door made of silk and dirt. Trap-door spiders spend the day inside with the door closed. At night, they raise the door and go out to trap insects.

A wolf spider is a very good hunter. It has **keen** eyesight and is able to move quickly. During the day, the wolf spider searches for insects. When it sees one, it races up and catches it.

Crab spiders move sideways slowly, just like crabs do. Crab spiders often trap and eat bees and butterflies. Sometimes they can change their body color to match what is around them. This helps them catch their food.

Can Spiders Harm People?

Few spiders are harmful to people. All spiders use their poison when they bite their prey. But their poison rarely harms people. Usually a spider bite just itches.

In North America, there are only six kinds of spiders that can harm people. The most dangerous is the black widow. This spider's poison is stronger than a rattlesnake's. The female black widow spider is the one that bites.

If you find a spider, look at it carefully. Count its legs. See its colors. Notice its beautiful web. Spiders are very interesting to watch!

23

Glossary

fangs pointed teeth

keen very, very good

poison harmful liquid

prey an animal eaten by another animal

silk a fine thread made by spiders

spinnerets where spiders make silk

tunnels underground pathways

weave to make by spinning threads

webs silk threads woven together by spiders